Five Feet

by

jd Watson

PublishAmerica
Baltimore

© 2004 by jd Watson.
All rights reserved. No part of this book may be reproduced, stored in a retrieval system or transmitted in any form or by any means without the prior written permission of the publishers, except by a reviewer who may quote brief passages in a review to be printed in a newspaper, magazine or journal.

First printing

ISBN: 1-4137-1335-1
PUBLISHED BY PUBLISHAMERICA, LLLP
www.publishamerica.com
Baltimore

Printed in the United States of America

DEDICATION

*For the enjoyment of those who like to read.
For the love of our parents who gave of themselves
to guarantee our future.
And for all our children, who will be responsible for our welfare,
as we grow older.*

ACKNOWLEDGMENTS

Much respect is due our elders, who have paved the way for us. Our parents and grandparents before them who gave their all to make the world a better place for us to live in. Yet many of our elderly are forgotten, they live alone, or in assisted living apartments, if not nursing facilities.

This book is fictional and derived from the life of our forgotten elderly. Many of our senior citizens live very isolated and lonely lives. So many times we hear reports in local and national newspapers of incidences similar to the one that Margaret Steaker finds herself in. Let this be a reminder to us all, just how much the weather conditions can take a toll on the lives of any community of senior citizens.

Many seniors are forgotten by their families and may have little or no contact from their loved ones. Oh sure, the yearly phone call and the occasional birthday card, is no substitute for a visit. The story of Margaret Steaker is an example of what can happen when we forget about our elderly loved ones. I would like to thank my family and friends for their strong, continued support for without them this book would not be possible. Thanks again.

Blessings ~ jd Watson

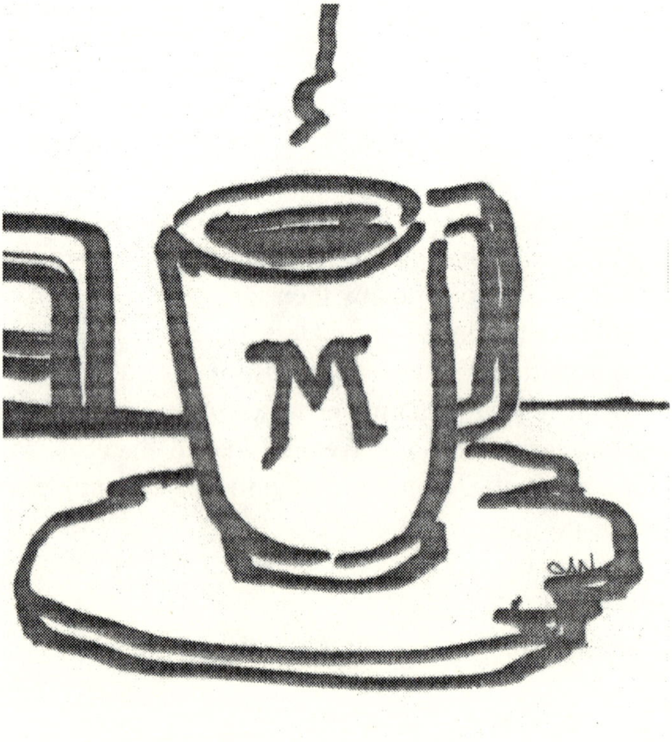
M

I

Sitting at the breakfast table, sipping the remains of her second cup of hot coffee, Margaret Steaker gazed through the partially opened curtains onto the blanket of snow that covered the backyard. Her eyes followed along the fence railing and up a big icicle that dangled from the garage gutter. The glistening snow sparkled like bits of glitter here and there. Yes the snow was beautiful she thought, yet she knew its dangers. The white, pristine, glistening blanket of snow had also kept her prisoner in her home several days at a time this winter. It was just mid February, and already six major snowstorms over the past three weeks. This year alone had record snow falls for this area.

As soon as the snowplows had cleared the streets the community braced itself for another storm it seemed. It was a never-ending event, the snowplows worked around the clock to keep the streets clear of snow. Neighborhood sidewalks were shoveled and swept by residents regularly in an effort to keep up with the snowfalls. The roaring snow blowers that Margaret's neighbors used, had blown mounds of snow in between street parking spots and the curb, never rested.

Margaret knew that complaining about the weather was no use. She had seen, over her lifetime, every type of weather imaginable. She thought about the time they all were snowed in for four days. School was closed, no buses ran, and the roads were closed. In fact you could only be on the road for an emergency, and if you were caught you would be ticketed and fined. Tom could not go to the office either. It was hectic keeping three young boys busy and Tom too. Fortunately the snow forts, ice skating and sleds kept them all out of the house and preoccupied. Margaret fixed the snacks and kept the gloves drying on the drying rack by the fireplace.

Margaret loved the old house and the wonderful times she had spent here. She and Tom had made it into a real home for the boys. She thought about the times severe thunderstorms and rain knocked the power off. The house was lit by candles. They would have to light candles and use flashlights to see, the boys thought it was like camping. *One time we did sing songs while we sat waiting for the power to be restored. Those were the days.*

Margaret loved to listen to the rainstorms and the muffled sounds the rain makes as each drop patters on the cushion of the rooftop. Margaret glanced at the fireplace in the living room that now remained silent. Margaret thought about the times she shared with Tom around the fire, talking, laughing, and drinking coffee. Tom liked to build a fire in the fireplace and Margaret would prepare some type of snack. Then the two of them nibbled on snacks and sipped coffee together as they watched the fire consume each log.

Margaret glanced up from her steaming cup of coffee and focused on the kitchen clock. Good she thought it was still early, 7:45 a.m. Margaret wanted to get an early start to the store to buy the essentials and gear up for the next snowstorm that was forecasted for that evening.

Margaret had done well this winter making sure she stocked up on things before the snow hit, that way she didn't have to go out in the severe weather. She wanted to prepare to be snowed in for a couple of weeks before running low on food and household needs. She kept the pantry stocked with soups and easy fix foods that didn't require a lot of cooking and preparation time. She bought foods that were packaged for small, individual servings. Margaret found cooking for one was tougher than cooking for the whole family. She was accustomed to cooking meals for five to eight people each meal. It was a real challenge to cook for just one.

Living at 1212 Madison Heights definitely had its advantages. Located in the heart of the suburb, they were located close to everything. When Tom and Margaret first moved to Madison Heights, there were few houses in the area, since then houses and residents have sprung up all over. Years before the nearest store was 30 minutes away, now with in 10-20 minutes, depending on traffic, Margaret could be at the store, church, the senior center, and just about most places that she needed to go. Most of her volunteer work was done at the local hospital not far away.

This winter touted numerous record snowfalls, the deepest was two weeks ago with a record 32 inches within a 24 hour period. That was the night Margaret stayed awake until the wee early morning hours, for the roar of the large salt trucks ran continuously through out the night. The city snow crew made every effort to clear the streets for early morning commuter traffic.

Another snowstorm system moving into the area was the last thought she wanted to entertain. Margaret thought back for a moment, for the past fall foliage had been a beautiful sight to behold. The artist, Mother Nature, had gracefully painted the rolling hillsides with vibrant golds, reds, oranges and greens. The past season held it delights for 79-year-old Margaret Steaker. It was the colors that stood out most in her mind. The past fall was one of the most colorful she recalled. The rustling of the leaves, the smell of wood burning in fireplaces were all too familiar, for she knew that it was the beginning of the autumn and winter seasons. Each season brings along pleasures and pains. Just as each brings about a unique beauty.

Thoughts raced through her mind of her late husband, Tom, and how they both enjoyed the changing of the seasons. She refilled her cup and stared across the empty kitchen table. She visualized her family, each in their spot, enjoying the morning meal. Those were certainly special times, when the whole family sat down for the meals. Margaret wondered just how many meals she had prepared in this kitchen, and the endless times that she and Tom had sat down together as husband and wife, sipping coffee while they discussed the upcoming events of the day. This had been her home for the past 57 years.

Margaret thought for a moment how hot the summer months of July and August can be in this area. The heat mixed with the humidity can seem twice as hot as it really is. Margaret remembered some hot summer nights before they had installed the air conditioning for the house, it was so hot that they camped out on sleeping bags in the backyard. That was just before little Bill was born. It was the fourth summer after they had moved there. The temperature was record setting for this area twenty-seven consecutive days of 100+ degrees breath taking heat. The heat wave was worldwide, and drought was everywhere. Thousands of people died throughout the world due to that heat wave. That summer was a special one for both she and Tom, for that was the time Margaret found out she was expecting her first child.

Margaret gave a mental flashback to the early morning weather report. For the weatherman had predicted that this new snow front was not due to roll in until late that evening. Another 8 to 10 inches was in the forecast for the area. Margaret looked towards the frosted window, she knew with all the latest technology in radar and weather tracking equipment, the local weathermen were quite accurate with their predictions. She peered at the heavy clouds that covered the sky. The gray blue overcast sky was customary in this area during the winter months.

Each season in the Midwest brought about that special excitement of the passing of time. It had been only three years since Tom had died and now the joy of fall, winter, or any of the seasons, did not hold the same emotions they once had. The tiny family of Margaret, Tom and their three sons, had dissolved. Since the boys had married, and moved far from the home place in Southern Illinois, Margaret now spent much of her time alone in the home she and Tom had made together. This particular winter had dropped more snow than any she could remember. Margaret had found herself snowed in for days upon end.

Cabin fever can be tough on anyone, yet Margaret kept busy and didn't really mind being snowed-in, so to speak. With the quilting and sewing, Margaret had little idle time. She busied herself with other handmade crafts, which she generously donated to various local charities. The quality of her quilts and crafts fetched a hefty price at the church bazaars and local fundraisers. Margaret prided herself in attention to detail and color co-ordinations in her sewing. She truly had the artistic flare for knowing which colors went together well and which didn't.

II

    Living independently had its ups and downs. True, there was the occasional visit from nearby neighbors, but other than that people pretty much minded there own business in the quaint suburb of Tipton. Margaret's sons tried to visit at least once a year, twice if things were in their favor, but things were different now that Tom was gone. Most of Margaret's time was spent alone. Now that the boys were grown with families of their own, and Tom, her husband passing away three years ago. Margaret now found her home empty. The walls no longer resounded the laughter, tears, and secrets it once held when Tom and the kids were still living there.
    Margaret was as meticulous about her sewing as she was her housekeeping. Everything was in its place, she kept the house very orderly and clean just in case she might have an unexpected visit from a neighbor or one of the boys and their families.
    Margaret stood up, walked to the back door and placed her index finger against the frosted windowpane. She thought of how much she loved snow, and especially on Christmas holidays. Margaret reminisced on those special Christmas Days when the snow pyramids and peaks covered each branch of the old apple tree, she now stared at, in the backyard. She looked up and down the trunk of the tree now with close to three feet of snow shrouding the knotty trunk. She could almost hear the bustling sounds in the background of the kids opening their Christmas presents, and rummaging through the large pile of gifts that engulfed the Christmas tree. She thought back to the first snow sleds that Tom had bought for the boys. Bright red, with planks of wood, Tom was more excited about the sleds than the boys were. That Christmas, Tom and the boys spent the day pulling and pushing the sleds through the backyard and around the same old apple tree she

now looked at.

That old apple tree had been a big part of the backyard scene for some time. Margaret remembered the day she and Tom planted the tree, it was barely two feet tall then. That apple tree was one of their first "home improvement" purchases the first year after they had bought the house. Tom said it would provide a suitable place to put a tree swing, plus it would provide good fruit for homemade pies and apple butter. Margaret smiled, and thought, Tom never got around to putting a swing in the tree, besides they bought a new swing set for the boys one summer while waiting on the tree to grow.

Being married for 55 years to the same person was wonderful. Tom was a great husband and father. He was such a family man and well liked by the local community. When Tom died from lymphoma cancer, Margaret felt that a part of her was buried along with Tom, for she had spent a big portion of her life with him by her side. But now only memories of the life they shared, their happiness, could only be seen in the family photos that lined the walls and the numerous photo albums, encased on the book shelves.

Margaret thought of how she and Tom had enjoyed a wonderful family life raising their three sons. With the boys involved in school activities and sports there was never a dull moment. There was always someone to pick up or an event to attend. In those days, Margaret spent many hours behind the wheel driving the boys to one activity or another. She remembered how happy she was when Bill, the oldest son, got his drivers license. Her chauffeuring excursion began to dwindle, for Bill was more than happy to take his younger brothers wherever they needed to go. She also remembered when Bill had asked to take the family car on his first real date with Susan Feldstein, his school sweetheart. Bill actually married that girl, Susan, and moved their family to the East Coast. New Jersey has been their home for the past 22 years.

Bill had become an air traffic controller, and he and Susan are the proud parents of two daughters. The oldest, Lisa, is expecting a child in late September of this year. The youngest, Sarah, will be graduating from college next year. Margaret thought about being a great-grandmother, she thought she might be a little too young for that. Now with the newcomer to the family Bill, her oldest son would be a grandfather this September. Margaret thought about the day that Bill was born and many special events throughout his life. His first day of school, the graduation from high school; it was hard to imagine his first grandchild.

Margaret's thoughts drifted onto Jesse, the middle son; he was always so independent and a true musician. Jesse had made California his home. After Jesse graduated from college his opportunity to teach music to young aspiring children soon landed him a job in California. Jesse had married Jenny Holder, a gal he met in college. Jesse and Jenny are both music majors, they met in graduate school. Jenny and Jesse both had great job opportunities in her hometown area in Orange County, on the West Coast. Jesse has two little boys. Ben is 12 and Tomas II is 9; they were both born in June. Tom was so happy when he found out the Jess was going to name one of his sons after him.

Jesse always did like music, even as a child he tried playing various instruments. He played instruments or sang songs all the time. Jesse had the lead role in several school plays and musicals. His talent rested in the arts. For his love of the arts and music was the driving force for his career and choices in life. *We even wall papered his bedroom with sheet music wallpaper design. At first I did not know if I would like it for that room but over the years I have adjusted.* It is the Fifth Major by Mozart. It was fascinating to hear him practice the wallpaper. He would invite the entire family in to hear his music recital. *Jesse is so theatrical, with a great sense of humor. He loves to read music and play different instruments.*

Edward, a biologist and the youngest, lives in Texas. He works for the Department of Science at the University of Texas. He married a professor who worked in the same department. Eddy and Marilyn have a 14-year-old daughter named Maggie and an 8-year-old son, Jonathan. Eddy loved the sciences, he was the son that toted spiders, snakes, and any other crawly thing that he could slip into his pocket to bring home.

Margaret smiled a hearty smile, for Eddy had a small zoo in his bedroom. His room looked much like a small laboratory with heat lamps and sun lamps for his different pets. There was the hamster, parakeet, gecko, rabbit, fish, snake and the turtle that all shared his room. Each had a name and was part of his little family.

One time they all spent hours trying to find a baby hamster that had got out of the cage and purportedly wandered too close to the snake's cage. Margaret smiled when she remember how funny it was with the whole family down on hands and knees frantically searching Eddy's room. Eddy had aquariums and terrariums everywhere. It was no surprise to anyone when Eddy majored in biology in school. That was his calling, so to speak.

Eddy lived the closest, just three states away. Yet Margaret felt a surge of contentment when little Edward could visit once a year instead of once every two or three years. All her sons had done well. Each had graduated from college, married and had families of their own. Each had successful careers ahead of them. Even though Margaret did not see her children or their families as much as she had liked to, she was happy knowing that each had found happiness in their lives. Even when Tom was alive, the boys were too busy to include frequent visits home. Once, maybe twice a year was the normal visiting allotment. Margaret thought that, women see their families more than men do in most marriages. All the boys were more involved, or closer to their wives' families than they were with their own birth family.

Thinking back Margaret smiled at the trying times she and Tom faced raising three boys only a year's plus difference in age between each. The squabbles, the sports, the dating, and the growing pains all added to the joy of parenting. Raising a family with a loving husband were the elements that made Margaret the happy mother and loving wife she was. Tom and Margaret joked frequently about the boys always having "hand me down" clothes for at one time they all pretty much wore the same sizes in pants, shirts and shoes. Margaret remembered buying all the same size underwear for the boys and dividing them equally among the three. It was not until junior high school that Eddy the youngest grew taller than his two older brothers, that is when Eddy could no longer wear his brother's clothes. Eddy is the tallest, he is 6'4", and he is tall like Tom. All the boys grew taller than Margaret, with Bill being 6' and Jess being 6'2."

FIVE FEET

Much had changed for Margaret in the past five years. With Tom's illness, the doctor visits, the long nights at the hospital, all had taken their toll on Margaret. The physical and emotional drain was intense. When Tom finally died three years ago, Margaret found herself left without the comforts and companionship of her husband. She had aged considerably and looked old and worn. Her face displayed a worn, wrinkled, worried look that was hard to wipe away. Margaret had so believed in Tom's full recovery. She believed Tom would be restored to good health. There was so much to live for. They had made so many plans of things that they were going to do, and places they were going to go. Tom's death was devastating to Margaret. She had lost a considerable amount of weight and now weighed a mere 102 pounds, which was thin for her 5' 5" medium frame.

Margaret soon realized that Tom was in fact terminal. It was one thing for Tom to die, and another was living through the agony and pain that led to his death. Watching her strong, healthy husband literally go from a man in every sense to a vegetable was almost more than anyone can sustain. The hardest thing for Margaret to grasp was when Tom no longer knew who she was, he did not recognize her nor did he know her name when she asked him. For hours upon end he spent his last few months strapped in a wheelchair staring down at the floor, drooling from the side of his mouth. Letting Tom go was just about all Margaret could take. It was very hard for her to bury her husband and the boys' father.

Now the two-story brick house that was once filled with laughter, tears and excitement was quiet and lonely, harboring only shadows and memories of days gone by. Each year it seemed harder and harder for Margaret to survive. Though financially there was no problem, being alone was difficult for Margaret. She had joined the Senior Citizens Club in town, and volunteered three days a week at the premature nursery at the hospital to help pass the time. In her spare time Margaret made quilts and crafts for the hospital's infant ward. There was always something to do or make.

One thing Margaret did enjoy was the fact that she was almost 80 and still had her driver's license and a fairly new car. With clear vision and good hearing, Margaret was very much in good physical condition for her age. This is one reason that she still lived in the local neighborhood at Tipton Creek subdivision. They all knew each other there, she had the same neighbors for years, with the occasional move-in, move-out by only two families since she and Tom bought the house 52 years ago.

This house almost seemed too much for her at times. Margaret made every effort to keep it up. She had hired a handyman that repaired, painted and restored the interior and exterior of the house. She had the entire house, inside and out, painted yearly, and had cleaning services visit every other week. Margaret was as meticulous about the house as she was her sewing. Everything was in its place. She dusted and swept daily just like when the kids were at home. Each room was orderly and neatly kept. Everything was in its place.

Each year brought about new challenges as the years went by. Walking up and down the stairs had become a challenge to Margaret. Without Tom there, Margaret rarely went upstairs where the boys' bedrooms were. It was funny Margaret thought how a big portion of her life was spent going up and down the 22 steps that led to the second story. The three bedrooms and a bath, were all that was up there. It was just enough to be home to the three boys who had lived there.

At first she and Tom thought about turning Bill's old bedroom into a study and Jesse's into a sewing room. They wanted to keep Eddy's room as the guest room. But they thought about the special times when the boys did visit or bring their families. It was nice for the boys to have their old rooms to sleep in.

Each of the three bedrooms reflected the interests and activities of the son that slept there. Everything was kept in its place, neat and orderly. It was as if time stood still in each room. For each room housed the same decorations it did while the boys were still in high school.

Bill's room, the "blue" room, was decorated with model airplanes and aviation gadgets. Margaret had made curtains out of fabric that had little airplanes printed on it. All the decorations and accessories were based on the aviation theme. That was Bill's choice. He loved airplanes and you could guess just by the way his bedroom was decorated. It looked like a private airplane hanger. Bill had model airplanes and remote planes all about the room. He had even hung two of his favorite models from the ceiling. Bill spent most of his free time putting together model airplanes or flying remote control model planes. Bill was totally absorbed with aviation, he knew the history as well. He kept up-to-date with the newest designs and technology. It was no surprise to anyone when Bill selected 'air traffic controller' as his career.

Jesse's room too was immaculate, it was decorated with sheet music wall paper. Anything and everything to do with music was found in Jesse's room. He had his favorite sheet music and lyrics blown up into poster size, framed and hung about his gallery. Jesse's room looked more like a high school band practice room. He had the latest recording equipment and tapes of his recitals and lessons. He played music any chance he could get. He played in two different rock bands while he was in college. He practiced faithfully all during high school and college. When he was selected for a four year scholarship to Huntington University, the number one music school in the US, the family was so proud of him they celebrated by throwing him a "going away" party with live music.

Eddy's room was decorated in animal and insect print curtains that Margaret had made. He had microscopes and science books of every sort on his bookshelves. The room that once resembled a miniature zoo now had only plastic molded animals. Eddy's bedroom still looked much like a jungle, with fake plants and animal specimens in every direction. Edward always had a love and passion for science. He loved animals and anything that had to do with biology.

III

With little use, now the second floor was all but closed off from the rest of the house. Margaret now found herself living on the ground level of the house with the kitchen, bedroom and bath conveniently located nearby; there was little need to go upstairs. Each boy's room had been left intact with the decorations and memorabilia that they had left behind. Margaret kept everything in its place so when the boys did return home for a visit, each could sleep in their old room and reminisce of the way things used to be during their childhood. It was much like they had never really left.

Feisty, independent and determined to live the rest of her life out in her home, Margaret was proud of the fact that she was still able to live independently. Other than regular maintenance and upkeep for odd jobs she could no longer do, Margaret did not ask for help. She resented the idea of moving into an apartment closer to town, or moving into the local assisted living facilities. She had always said she would live at home as long as she could take care of herself, for this is where she was the happiest, on her own at her own home.

For the past five years, Margaret had done volunteer work for St. Mary's Hospital, which was a ten minute drive away. She enjoyed her work at the hospital, it was a chance to get out and do something worthwhile. Margaret had begun working there as a full-time volunteer shortly after Tom's death. Working with premature infants in the maternity ward was especially rewarding for her. Working three days a week was just enough to keep Margaret busy. She drove to work, and even packed her lunch so that she could sit with other staff and visit during the lunch hour. She was well liked and most people called her "Granny" at the hospital. Several of the staff had met her during Tom's cancer treatments. Her frequent visits and overnight stays with Tom at

St. Mary's gave her the opportunity to get acquainted with doctors, nurses, orderlies and cleaning staff. When one of Tom's nurses recommended Margaret apply for the volunteer program, she jumped at the chance to work at St. Mary's as a full-time volunteer. This kept her busy and gave her something to look forward to each week. Margaret loved her volunteer work at the hospital.

In Margaret's spare time she quilted baby blankets for the hospital's newborn babies and donated them to the many families in need. She bought fabric remnants from the local fabric store and quilted baby quilts of bright colored patchworks. Margaret had prided herself with the opportunity to give back to the hospital in any way that she could. Making the little quilts was something she enjoyed doing. She paid careful attention to use bright colors: reds, blue, and yellows, with differing hues of each. She gave the red-pink quilts to the little baby girls and the blues to the boys. The yellows could be used for either. Each little quilt was different with colorful quilt patterns. Sometimes she used the star pattern, other times she used a pinwheel pattern that looked like connecting flowers.

After Tom's death, Margaret had also joined the Tipton's Senior Citizens Center. It was just minutes away and was the local meeting place for the community seniors to gather. There were about thirty regulars. Some were married couples, singles, and widows who visited the center daily. They were considered the non-residents who could come and go as they pleased. The seniors center also had a wing that housed forty-two residents who lived there and required various levels of care. Many of the residents required Skilled Level 4 nursing care, or basically around-the-clock monitoring. The center provided hot meals for all senior citizens, at a fraction of the actual cost. Non-residents frequented the center for balanced hot meals, socialization and something to do all day. There was always a game of bingo, checkers, or cards going on in the activity room. The center also sponsored crafts, sing-a-longs, church, movies and field trips for both residents and non-residents to attend. It was a pretty good deal for seniors with lots of time on their hands.

Margaret did not feel as if she were a senior citizen. She did not want to live at the center, nor did she want to spend a lot of idle time there. Margaret kept busy helping in any way that she could. She volunteered to teach craft classes at the center to help the program director with activities for the community of seniors. When she did go to the senior center she helped and stayed busy helping others. The staff and participants just loved Margaret. Many knew her by name, they knew the boys, and Tom. Some of the staff went to school with the boys and remembered Margaret from their youthful days.

Over the past two months, Margaret had limited her visits to the senior citizens center. She had much in common with many of the seniors there. It was true that most of the seniors shared the same age, married or widowed, and all had witnessed the past years from youthful eyes. But for Margaret the visits left her feeling old and lost. She did not like seeing people her age barely able to get around, and needing the level of care that many of the elderly there required. At times, Margaret's visits to the senior citizens center were all but depressing. It merely served as a reminder of what life's final turn has in store. Margaret knew that she was truly one of the lucky ones to still be living on her own, driving, able to cook and take care of herself. She was all but totally independent.

IV

    This winter was an especially trying one. There had been frequent snows, ice storms, and exceptionally cold, unseasonable weather. The preceding fall gave no indication of what lie in store for this winter. The cold was taunt and disturbing. There were several days that Margaret found herself at home alone, for the harsh weather had predicated the coming and going of everyone. Margaret could only think how long this winter would last. She could not volunteer as much as she wanted, nor could she drop in at the senior center. She had completed several new craft ideas she wanted to share with the center's program director for craft classes. Yet the recent snowstorms had restricted all commuter traffic of this suburbia community.

    The roads were kept quite clear with snow plowed to the curbs for essential passage. It was not the street but rather each house's drive and walkway that presented the biggest obstacles. Cabin fever had struck most locals, who hurriedly rushed to the local market stocking up on necessary supplies before each storm hit. Margaret had found herself, like many others, stocking up on essential at the local supermarket, awaiting the next rash wave of bad weather. At times Margaret found herself spending 3-4 days snowed in, only able to move from room to room in her world of memories.

    This day was no different, cold and more snow on the way! With weary fingers, Margaret pulled back the heavy winter drapes and peered out a frosty coated front room picture window. The neighborhood now looked like a "winter wonderland" with snow-covered trees, shrubs, flower beds, rooftops, and cars. The sidewalks were shoveled with occasional signs of drifted snow.

    Margaret smiled and thought of the boys sledding down the hill in the back of their property. She remembered it was more like a neighborhood gathering place when it snowed. Just at the end of their backyard, where several proposed building lots had not yet been sold, there nestled between adjoining property lines, stretched a gentle hill, ideal for sledding. This little hill ran the entire block. When it snowed, all the neighborhood kids came armed with sleds, tire inner tubes, or anything that would slide, accompanied by dogs, puppies and other pets; laughter filled the air for hours. Up and down, back up and then down the kids would go, with the dogs trailing, or riding with the kids.

For the boys, 'snow days' proved to be an endless cycle, either sliding down or towing their ride back to the top. Tom was just as much a kid as the boys were. He would be right with them sliding down the hill, playing in the snow, helping with the snow forts and the occasional snowball fights. Margaret was used to that, Tom playing along with the boys, he was very close to all of them. Her job then was to make sure there was plenty of hot chocolate, cookies to replenish lost energy and have a pair or two of dry gloves readily available for whoever got wet or cold.

On this day, the 11th of February, Margaret knew that it was cold outside. The chilling cold that came with this winter was colder than any winter that Margaret could remember. The wind chill factor had caused temperatures to plummet into the minuses, with a blanket of snow that had encased the surrounding area for the past three weeks. This year provided more snow and ice than any of the previous years. Margaret knew that a new blizzard was soon approaching the area with the possibility of six-seven inches of new snow expected to add to the twelve inches they already had accumulated from previous snows. She was happy that her neighbor, Henry Goldstein's son Ben, had cleared her walkway promptly after each snow.

Ben was such a helpful young man. He had moved in two doors down in the ' old home place,' after his parents Henry and Kathy had passed away. For the past two years Ben and his little family had inhabited the Goldstein's family residence. Ben was two years younger than Edward and was one of the neighborhood kids that frequented the house playing games and watching movies with the boys. Ben helped a lot of the old folk still left in the neighborhood complete the everyday and seasonal chores. He was always there to clear the snow, rake leaves, prune bushes, and mow lawns.

Ben had married one of the girls he went to high school with, and they are expecting their first child. Being an only child, Ben had inherited the family home, and now had made it his family home. Ben taught math at the same high school he and the boys had attended years before.

Thoughts of spring raced through Margaret's mind. Memories of the kids and Tom put a smile on her face. "Each season brings forth its pleasures," she whispered as she drew back from the cold of the window. She tugged at the drapes and backtracked to the kitchen for another cup of coffee.

Margaret was happy to enjoy the cold for she knew it would not last forever. She recaptured the weatherman's report in her mind. The blizzard would not be upon her until much later that evening. She knew that she had time to run to the store and stock up on some of the bare necessities: milk, bread, and her medical prescription needed to be filled. She was down to three sleeping pills, and wanted to refill before this next storm front moved in. Just barely 10 minutes from town and the local market, Margaret prepared to venture out before the storm was scheduled to arrive.

A quick shower and clothes would be all that was needed to be on her way. Margaret fumbled through the dresser drawer and found her black polyester slacks, then went to her clothing chest and got her pink blouse and slipped it on. Now dressed and ready to go, Margaret thought about her red sweater but realized it would probably be too bulky under the raincoat, plus she had planned to be back in a few minutes anyway. No need to overdress, the heater in the car worked wonders, even on low.

Margaret had bought the car only three years ago, it was in good condition, and regularly maintained. She had just bought new tires, not because the car needed them but because she wanted the safety of new snow tires for the winter. Margaret had put ten thousand miles on the car, driving short distances only. The Chevy, as she called it, was in excellent working condition and ran great. The car was still under warranty.

Margaret knew that she was one of the lucky ones still able to live on her own. She could come and go as she pleased with valid drivers license. She thought about the residents at the senior's center. Many were doomed to a life in a wheelchair. Others could not feed themselves, or take care of their basic needs. She thought how lucky she was to be able to get around as well as she does. She could cook her own meals, drive to the store, pay her bills and still take care of her two-story house. Margaret was happy that she still was able to do for herself.

Margaret was not worried for she had made the trip to the store numerous times before. She was not afraid to drive in snow or icy conditions because she had just bought new snow tires for the car only two months earlier. The snow had been plowed and the roads were cleared, and besides she had left the car in the driveway just a short walk from the door.

Margaret looked through the closet and grabbed the first coat she saw. It was her thin off-white raincoat with the zip-in liner. She knew this raincoat was a good water repellant. Margaret slipped her arms through the sleeves and pulled it upon her shoulders. Next she grabbed her black vinyl boots. She knew these boots were not very good on ice but worked wonders in the snow plus the fur lining added extra warmth. Sitting on the edge of the bed and lifting her tiny feet, she slipped into her boots and peered down at them. She had these boots for years. Tom had bought them for a Christmas present years ago.

A hat, purse and gloves were all that she needed to complete her accessories, after all she would just be gone a few minutes, from a warm house, to the car and into the stores. A maximum of 25 minutes was all that it would take and she would be back in the comforts of her home, ready to ride out the on coming snow storm. Margaret knew she had plenty of time to spare before the upcoming snow and would be back home in plenty of time before the first flakes were scheduled to fall. The weatherman had said it wouldn't start snowing until late that evening, it was barely 9:42 a.m. as she glanced at the wall clock for confirmation. She would be back home by 10:30 a.m. at the latest. The trip was short and routine.

FIVE FEET

    Margaret thought of times in the past when she would go out into unseasonably cold weather. A hat was most important because it would keep almost 80 percent of her body heat in. She rummaged through her drawers and found her favorite hat and pulled it securely on her head. The gray one with the white rabbit fur trim was a favorite winter hat for Margaret, Tom had bought it for her. In fact it was the last gift she would receive from her then dying husband.
    Looking in the mirror, Margaret thought of the memories of her life gone by. Her hair no longer golden was now white, as white as the snow she would soon venture into. Her face held many of her tales of days gone by. With thin lines and wrinkles, it now carried the story of the joyous life she had lived. Her brown eyes now seemed grayish-blue from age. She smiled and thought of Tom and the kids. Her life had been near to perfect. She grabbed the car keys from the dining room table and with that she walked to the front door, opened it, sleeked out and closed the door behind her and began her mad dash to the car.

V

    Margaret immediately realized how cold it truly was, for the brutally cold wind pierced the pores on her face. It was indeed much colder than she had thought. The sky was overcast, with clouds announcing the oncoming storm. Margaret looked up at the sky. She knew that it promised more snow and bone-chilling weather. Margaret thought about the cold air, for if she had known it was actually this cold she would have grabbed her scarf to wrap around her face.

    Each breath brought a stinging coldness to her lungs. The air was bitter as she inhaled, almost taking her breath away. Margaret peered out at the front yard blanketed in the soft white snow before her. She heard the distant sound of muffle salt trucks spreading salt and sand the next street over. She knew that it would not be long before they roared down the street she lived on.

    Margaret thought of the numerous trips that the salt trucks had already made this winter. She looked up to the heavy overcast gray-blue sky and knew that the next snowstorm would soon be on its way. She pulled her shoulder bag tightly upon her shoulder. With a sudden gush of wind, Margaret grabbed her flapping coat and pulled it closely to her body. It didn't really matter how cold it actually was, she thought, for she knew she would be in the car in a few more steps, and that would block the wind and its chilling factor. Then on to the store and back before you know it. Just a few minutes was all that it would take.

FIVE FEET

The wind chill factor certainly makes it feel a bit colder than it really is, Margaret thought.

Margaret was glad that she had left the car parked in the drive, just a mere five feet from the walkway and she would be sitting in the driver's seat ready to go in seconds. Just a few more steps and then she would be in the car, she reminded herself, for the wind had picked up and needled its way through her thin coat. Margaret could feel the frigid cold, she was getting cold. The wind's force was strong and caused the coat to fly open. Margaret held fast the coat flaps, as the coat would not stay buttoned with the wind pulling at it. She found herself giving to the force of the wind, she could not walk a straight line; the wind, her coat, her boots, were all opposing every effort she made towards the car.

Margaret glanced ahead at the new tires and the cleared driveway. Ben had used his little garden tractor's snow blade to clear the snow from behind the car. Margaret thought how kind Ben was to keep the snow plowed from her walkway and drive. He had been so helpful this year.

Again the brutal wind gained momentum and blew her coat, parting it at the last button. She thought a moment and pushed forward, maybe she should have worn her heavy winter coat. The frigid cold had pierced the raincoat's lining, she pushed the thought from her mind. For she would only be gone just a few minutes to the store and back, no need to overdress, she would be in the car in a few more steps. Margaret's doubting thoughts played over and over in her mind as she stared at the car door, and glanced down at the new tires.

The daunting thoughts returned to Margaret. Maybe she should have worn several layers of clothes. Or maybe she should not try to go out in this frigid cold, nonsense! She pulled the coat up closer around her tiny frame, and tugged at the collar to block the cold air from her face. Her nose now cold and dripping, it was much colder than she had realized. The bitter wind caused her to blink her eyes excessively which still provided no protection from the cold. Margaret felt as if she was swimming upstream, it was as if each step she struggled against the forces of the wind and coldness.

Being 5 foot 5 inches, weighing 102 pounds at her age was something Margaret prided herself in. True she had lost weight shortly after Tom died, but she did not miss the extra pounds. She was happy that she had kept her weight down and retained her youthful agility, she was in perfect physical and mental condition. At her most recent check-up the doctors had given her a complete physical and raved at her good health condition. They had only prescribed a mild sedative to help her fall asleep at night. Margaret had trouble falling asleep at nights, just since Tom had died. She wanted the prescription to help her get the rest she needed.

VI

Just a few more steps and she would be there, the brutal cold bit again through the raincoat and flapped the sides against the polyester slacks as she staggered from the forces of the wind. She thought of all the people her age who had just let themselves go, many overweight and unable to get around. Several of her friends were confined to wheelchairs, and others had to utilize metal walkers just to get around. Some of her friends were living at the assisted living center or the nursing home, unable to care for themselves. Margaret thought how fortunate she was to be able to live on her own.

Now the car was but a mere five feet away, Margaret was feeling the excitement of living independently. The thought of being able to drive herself to the store, and the freedom of living on her own, in a few more steps, that freedom would be fully exercised and realized as she would start the car and drive herself to the store. The wind whipped from around the side of the house. It was getting colder.

Without notice, the black ice underfoot gave no warning of the slippery conditions. It was as if Margaret was falling in slow motion, her feet flew from under her body. All her weight was now being hurdled through the air as she landed only five feet from the car. Startled, cold, and shaken and so close, Margaret now lay in a contorted shape on the sidewalk. She knew from the excruciating pain that she had broken a bone in her leg, ankle, or hip, at this point she was not sure exactly where the pain was coming from. As hard as she tried to get up, she could not manage to stand. The walkway was unforgiving and frozen from the cold. Margaret looked at herself in the reflection on the ice. Her hands were cold and clenched in fists. The freezing cold shot through her legs and into her hips.

Thoughts raced through Margaret's mind. One minute she was just about to reach the car door handle, and the next minute she was lying on the ground with unbearable pain shooting up her leg and spine. Margaret bit her lip. "What happened?" she moaned for the pain she was now experiencing could not be mistaken, it was a broken hip. "How could this be?" She had always been so careful. She had lived the past three years alone here at this house, she knew the ins and outs of being single living here. How could she not see that black ice? Living in this area, in the Midwest, you always assume that the walkways are slippery when snow was on the ground. That was a rule of thumb. Margaret thought back for a moment, fumbling with the coat was throwing her off balance while she walked, that is how she lost her balance on the ice.

Analyzing the situation was not enough to change her present condition. No matter how much Margaret reasoned with herself she could not manage to lift her body from the cold surface of the sidewalk. The pain from the broken hip dictated her movements. She realized that she would have to try every way she could to get up from the frozen surface soon, for she could feel the cold seeping into her limbs.

For a moment Margaret laid there staring at the new tires on the car. Her tiny frame lay hidden by the snow piled on each side of the walkway. No one could see her as she lay helplessly on the ground. The colors of her clothing blended well with the white blanket of snow and the snow-covered shrubs. Her white hair blended perfectly with the surrounding snow. Her silhouette was camouflaged into small mounds of snow. Her favorite gray hat, with the white rabbit fur, looked naturally placed with the snow engulfing the hood for it had landed in the snow just inches out of Margaret's reach.

At that moment time stood still for the 79-year-old Margaret Steaker. For what seemed like hours had passed as Margaret made futile struggles to get up from the frozen ground. No matter how hard she tried, she could not get her feet under her body. The black ice that had been her initial demise was now her captive. She could not gain any traction on the ice, and the ice span engulfed the width of the walkway. She was surrounded by the ice. She could not get a grip with her hands, nor could she get any traction with her feet. Each time she placed her 'working foot' underneath her, it slid, twist sharply inward and sent her body slapping abruptly to the frozen surface. The moment she tried to put any support or pressure on it, she would begin to slide in the direction of the broken hip. Margaret tried to get up on her hands and knees, but her legs would slide on the ice from under her, sending her to the walkway with a dull thud sound. She could only lift herself inches above the slick, icy surface. She could not get any traction on the ice.

Margaret dug at the ice with her gloved hands, she thought she would have better luck if she took her gloves off. Maybe she could get a grip on the ice and pull herself to the edge and roll over to the edge of the walkway into the snow and pull herself on the hardened snow. Margaret put her left hand to her mouth and bit the end of the glove that covered her index finger, pulling the glove free from her hand. She repeated the action and did the same for her right hand. With both hands free she tried effortlessly to grab a hold of the ice. Margaret tried as hard as she could to pull herself closer to the car. Everything was working against her. Her fingers were now numb from the ice and wind. She could not get them unclenched. The air was freezing cold. Margaret scrambled to find her gloves, both were now out of reach. She tried to bury her freezing fingers in her coat, but she could not lift herself enough to do so.

Margaret tried to roll over, but with the broken hip the maneuver was impossible. Each time she rocked to her left side, the pain stifled her movement. She tried to roll onto her right side, but the broken appendage would not allow it. Margaret lay as if pinned to the ice by a heavyweight wrestler. She had used all her energy to no avail. She could not get up from the sheet of ice. The sidewalk was brutally frozen and enhanced the tingling effects of the onset of hypothermia.

Something was broken, she could tell by the sound and the way she landed, something was surely broken. Margaret's greatest fear had been realized, from the excruciating pain, she knew her hip bone had snapped from the sudden fall. All 102 pounds had landed on her left side, right below her pelvic bone. Her head was now bare as her hat lay but inches away from her reach. Margaret's left leg simply would not work, she could not get it positioned underneath her to hold her weight. With a broken limb as such, escaping this peril was next to impossible.

Helplessly sprawled on the frozen ground, she lay calling out to no one but the wind as trees spoke softly from each branch bending like synchronized dancers. No one was out in this frigid cold. No one could see the tiny body laying five feet from the car. No one could hear Margaret's pleading calls for help, for the howls of the rustling wind consumed the air and dominated the sounds of winter.

From the street the snow neatly piled on the walkway prevented, what few passersby that drove by from seeing the tiny figure helplessly struggling to get up from the frozen ground. Nor could the neighbors see Margaret frantically fighting to regain her footing. No one could see over the mounds of snow. For the snowplows had banked snow in cascading piles, sporadically along the street, blocking everyone's view. Margaret could not see over the snow piles from where she lay. She could not get her arms in a position to wave or flag someone's attention. Margaret knew there was little chance of surviving her fate. A chilling numbness slowly settled in her lower extremities. The ice would be her tomb, there was no escape.

VII

With a gush of the chilling wind, softly and gently large fluffy snowflakes swirled to the ground, each landing gracefully at its personal resting place. Of the millions of snowflakes, no two are alike. Each has a destiny, a direction, and their own individual life. Some snowflakes grow as they pass through the layers of sky. Others dissipate before they reach the ground. Yet other snowflakes pile, layer upon layer, coating, blanketing the earth below. Snow hides the iniquities of humans, some say it covers all sinfulness. For no one knows what lies beneath the snow.

The snow blizzard had come earlier than predicted. Margaret was not sure how long she had been lying on the ground. She guessed it had been over an hour; her legs, feet, and fingers were now numb and seemed all but frozen, she knew that she had no feeling in most of her body. She could barely feel the snow that had melted and coated her face with a thin layer of ice. Margaret was not cold, she felt the warmth of the snow as it covered her with a light fluffy blanket, it felt just like her soft flannel blanket she had on the bed.

Thoughts raced through Margaret's mind. She thought about the thin coat she had just taken from the closest just minutes before. For now she wished she had taken time to get her heavy winter coat. She thought about the hat that now lay outside her reach, her head exposed and now, snow gently cascading down, she was covered. It no longer melted on her exposed skin. Margaret felt warm and comfortable.

Margaret focused on the snow that blanketed her body. Each snowflake is individually sculptured in the air as it drifts towards the earth. Margaret wondered how many individual snowflakes it took to cover a square yard area, and how many had landed on her. She always loved a fresh blanket of snow that covered everything and made everything look clean, peaceful and serene.

Margaret thought of the times she and Tom would walk around the block in a late night snow. The crunchy sound of fresh snow as their boots broke the innocent, pristine white carpet. The moonlight reverberated off the white snow, radiating light all around. It was like a muffled daylight when the moon is full and the night is clear. You can see quite a distance, Margaret remembered.

She could no longer feel the pain of her hip. Her hands felt numb and useless. Margaret lay still as the snow continued to drift down upon her. She watched as large, delicately formed flakes of snow swirled in erratic patterns high above her head before they found their place of rest. This was a heavy snowstorm, accumulating fast on anything in its path.

The weatherman was wrong. Margaret played that thought over and over in her mind. The weatherman had forecasted the snow to begin in the late evening, yet it was not mid-day and already a inch and a half of snow had fallen. She had placed a lot of faith in getting accurate weather predictions on the early morning news. The Channel 3 News was usually pretty accurate, she recanted. Yet this time Margaret knew in her heart that the storm had came much sooner than predicted. She was caught in the snowstorm.

What was she thinking of, trying to get out on a day like this? For no one in their right mind would have tried to venture out in weather like this. She thought of the car, so close yet so far away, if she could have only made it five feet further she would have made it. She stared at the new tires she had bought just months ago. She was so close, if only she could move her legs, maybe she could possibly crawl to the car. Maybe she could somehow crawl back to the house, but it seemed further away than the car.

The snow continued to fall, the wind howled as it blew snow from housetops to the ground. Margaret could fight no longer; she was exhausted and sleepy. Margaret knew that she had struggled for at least the last two hours to no avail. She was not sure if it was day or late evening, with an overcast cloudy sky it is hard to tell what time of day it was. She knew that what once seemed cold, now seemed not to matter,

FIVE FEET

for she was beginning to feel a sudden warmth rush through her body. Though she had no sensation now in the entire left side of her frail body, she felt relaxed and comfortable. The struggle to call out, to regain her footage, had ceased.

Margaret's mind flashed back to her sixth birthday party. She could remember it so vividly. She was finally turning six years old. She was Daddy's little princess. It was Margaret's first real birthday party that she was allowed to invite her school mates from first grade. Mom had helped her write the invitations and Dad helped with the games. Margaret's two older brothers, Michael and William were there too. Susan was not born yet. Everyone helped with the party and the games. There were big bunches of colorful balloons, party hats, with plenty of chocolate cake and ice cream. She remembered the pretty yellow gingham dress that she wore. She remembered the big chocolate cake that had her name on it. She thought about all the six candles that were placed randomly on the thick icing. That was really a special day for her. It was a party that she could never forget.

Margaret thought about the times she walked to the local store to buy candy after she had gathered all the pop bottles she could find to return for a cash deposit. Five cents per bottle was no laughing matter in those days. The price would fetch a hefty bag of candy. As a child Margaret had a sweet tooth; she loved to eat candy and was willing to collect empty soda bottles to sell for the deposit money so she could buy candy. Mom and Dad didn't buy much candy, and besides Margaret's older brothers were big eaters. It took all the family could muster just to keep enough food on the table.

Margaret could hear the big snowplow truck as it rounded the corner. Louder and louder the sound grew coming within yards of where she now lay. She tried as hard a she could to raise her hand in a last 'ditch effort' to flag down the now approaching truck. No such luck, she couldn't position herself to get her limbs to respond. The scraping sounds of the snow blade soon faded deep into a distant hush, as the snow continued to fall.

Margaret's thoughts shifted to her mother, how strong, and inspirational her mother had been. Margaret's mother was a housewife.

She kept the house and raised four children. She cooked all the meals, did all the washing, ironing, and ran the daily household. Margaret remembered how her mother worked very hard, doing laundry for the neighbors to make extra spending money. Margaret's mom and dad were good parents. They wanted the best for their children. They were very supportive of Margaret going to college. In those days, girls didn't go to school beyond high school, they usually married and became housewives. Margaret was the first woman in her family to complete a college education. It was a big deal when she did finally graduate.

VIII

Thoughts of Margaret's life rapidly flashed through her mind as if none of the details were spared. She thought of the wonderful life she had lived. Tom and the kids, yes she had been a good wife. She knew in her heart that she had been a wonderful mother to her three sons. She thought about all the newborn babies in the hospital's premature ward and how much she enjoyed rocking them and cradling them in the tiny quilts she had made. Each new baby had a special place in her heart. Oh how the joy flowed when they left the hospital for home. Margaret loved to see the expressions of joy the proud parents had for their new addition to their family. She reflected back on the day she and Tom brought each of their sons home from the hospital.

With Bill being the first child, everything was new for Margaret and Tom. Margaret could remember Tom jokingly saying, "I wish they would send instructions on how to take care of a newborn attached to the baby's blanket," with that they both laughed.

Margaret reflected back to memories of the past.

"I, Margaret Elizabeth Straton, was born to Mary and James Straton. I am originally from the small town, of Williamsburg. Williamsburg, Indiana is in the southeastern-most part of the state. I was the third child in a family of four. I had two older brothers, Michael and William respectively, and one younger sister, Susan. My dad worked for the railroad. In those days believe me, that was considered top of the line employment. My mom did not work outside of the home until my little sister Susan was out of high school. My mother spent her life raising us four kids. I attended the local elementary school, Williamsburg Elementary on the south side of Williamsburg. I went on to high school, and graduated from Belmont High School."

Margaret reminisced for a moment and began to mutter, "When I was eight years old, I was in the third grade. At that time I happened to be one of the best spellers in the class. There were numerous times that I won the class spelling bee. One of my most embarrassing moments was misspelling the word 'be.' I wanted to make it harder than it was. I just could not remember how to spell it. This was so embarrassing because it only has two letters in the word. I can still remember the look on a puzzled Mrs. Garrett when I was unable to spell such a simple word. What made this extra embarrassing was that Mrs. Garrett was my teacher and my Girl Scout leader too. I looked up to her in many respects. I thought the world of her. I always knew she was shocked I could not spell that word, it was so simple.

"That is one thing Tom and I agreed on the boys would be in the local Scout program and we both were active leaders and supporters." Margaret began showing signs of confusion and disorientation. She began talking as if someone was there to hear her. She jumped back and forth in time and confused events.

Growing up in Williamsburg, for Margaret, had its advantages and disadvantages. Everyone knew everyone, it is pretty much small town living there. "It was big news when I left for college in another state. Most kids I graduated with went to the local Williamsburg Community College for a two-year degree and then found local jobs, many carrying on the family business or working in their family's rural agricultural business farms. Margaret could hear the distant sounds of summer. Birds chirping, crickets singing and tree frogs bellowing. She could smell the fresh fragrance of blooming rose bushes seeping through the kitchen window.

"My two brothers still live in Williamsburg. My brother Michael, the oldest, has three children by his second wife and my brother William has two children. Michael has grandchildren, and great grandchildren.

We all have grandchildren now."

Margaret seemed to drift in and out of consciousness. One moment she thought of her immediate situation, lying five feet from the car on the frozen ice slick sidewalk, slowly freezing to death. Her next thoughts would carry her throughout the events of her lifetime.

"Growing up in a small town atmosphere was great. Williamsburg is 22 miles west of the tri-state area where Indiana, Ohio, and Kentucky all join together. Mom and Dad lived in the Williamsburg area all their lives. Being raised in the Williamsburg area, I knew all the neighborhood kids by name. We all played together, went to the same school and went to the same church on Sundays. We were expected to marry 'the girl/guy next door.' I was a cheerleader from sixth grade to varsity in high school. Everyone knew me as Michael and William Straton's little sister." Cold air rushed to fill Margaret's lungs, as she gasped at the freezing brutal bitterness. She tried to pull the coat closer around her neck, but her hands would not obey her. She did not realize both arms now lay lifeless against the frozen ground.

Margaret rambled on in a muffled voice, "My best friend lived next door to my house. Her name was Cassie Globe. I can remember people were always teasing Cassie because of her name. Cassie and I walked to school every day hand in hand, laughing, telling stories of the latest television show. We were best of friends until high school, when we both started taking different directions with our lives. Cassie was married at the sweet age of 16, I guess that was acceptable seventy years ago, people married young, plus Cassie was with child. Back in those days you didn't have the choices that people have today. When you got pregnant, you got married. Most of it was just to give the kid a name. Like most teenage marriages, Cassie and her husband end up living with the in-laws for the first few years. Cassie dropped out of school, and I never saw much of her after that, other than the occasional run-in at the local market. Let me think, yes it was a year or so later, after Cassie had the baby, a baby girl. Yes that's right, Cassie had a little girl, her daughter was about two years old then.

"I haven't been back to Williamsburg for a while. I still get Christmas cards from my brothers and their families each year. Tom and I tried to go back there each year and take the kids. I guess William, my youngest brother, has had a lot of trouble with his youngest son getting into trouble. The courts gave him fifteen years for an armed robbery that they claimed he was not in on. I hear the boy drove his friends to a local store for sodas, and they went in and robed the store while William's boy waited outside in the car, thinking his friends went in only for sodas. I would say, he was in the wrong place at the wrong time, and ended up losing fifteen years of his life for it.

"My oldest brother Michael is expecting his seventh grandchild. His daughter is due to give birth sometime this spring. Michael has been the one to keep the family name going with so many sons, he just has the one daughter. Melissa is her name, she married a fellow out of New York. I was surprised that a person from New York would settle for living in Williamsburg Indiana, but now I see the attraction, of a big city person, moving to a small town, rural area."

Margaret thought about how excited she was to be selected to sing in the fifth grade choir. "Mr. Harris…hmm…yes that was his name. Mr. Harris was the choir director and the music director for the elementary students. He had a slight lisp in his speech, but he taught us a lot of really great songs, like 'No Man is an Island,' and 'The Sound of Music.' Those were my favorite songs at that time. Williamsburg Elementary housed grades K-8, from there you went on to Belmont High School. There were five elementary schools but only one high school." Margaret's hallucinations sent her walking down the hallways of Belmont High.

"It was so funny going to high school in Williamsburg, you may be a cougar, a falcon, dragon or a cardinal in elementary school, but when you went to Belmont High School you were an 'Eagle.' Belmont Eagles, we had one of the best football teams in the area. The Belmont Eagles won sectionals the four years that I attended there. I was on the Varsity Cheer-block Pep club. I went to all the games and cheered the Eagles. Margaret envisioned a brown paper bag, overflowing with buttered popcorn clutched in her right hand, accompanied by a small cup brimming with coke in her left.

"My younger sister Susan moved to Linton, 75 miles south of

Williamsburg, after her graduation from business college. Susan is a secretary and has worked for the city in Linton all her life. She has three sons. She married a guy who she met in Linton named Bill Burch, and they have been there every since. She comes to Williamsburg now and then to see Mom and Dad." The wind had somewhat subsided. The snow continued to blanket the shrubs, housetops and Margaret.

"It was a real change for me when my little sister came along, for almost nine years I was the only girl in the Straton family and then along came Susan. For all those years before I was Daddy's "little princess," that is what he called me. Having older brothers and being the only girl in the family had its advantages and disadvantages. Mom and Dad were overly protective of me. I lived a very sheltered life. I did not go on my first date until I was 17 years old. I was expected to be a role model for little Susan. Having a sister nine years younger than you is just like being born a built-in babysitter. Mom and Dad were a lot more lenient on Susan than they were on me. Susan being the baby of the family got away with more things than I ever did. That didn't really bother me, I left for college when Susan was 10 years old. It was great to have a little sister." Margaret could smell the fresh baked cinnamon rolls her mother had just pulled out of the oven, her mind had provided her an escape from the immediate perils of death.

"Susan passed away eight years ago. She died an unexpected death with massive heart failure. She left behind four children: two boys and two girls. All Susan's children still live in the Linton area. Susan had eight grandchildren. Out of all the family Susan had the most children. The last I saw any of Susan's kids was at her funeral. I was surprised to see all her children and grandchildren there. There was a slew of hers and Bill's relatives there. It must be late, probably around midnight. The sun is shining very bright tonight." Margaret's exposed skin, now encased in a thin layer of ice, no longer melted the encroaching snow.

IX

"I can clearly remember the first day Tom Steaker and I met. It was a cold, snowy Super Bowl Sunday, January 26th. Mutual friends of ours, Benny and Sarah Lewis had planned the perfect Super Bowl party. The game, the people, and the setting were all in good taste. The spirit of the game was overwhelming as we all joined in to talk about play by play. Sarah had planned the perfect pitch-in. The different variety of foods, harmonized to be a nice spread. The food was nothing but excellent, and the company was great. We all sat glued to the television watching every move as we all munched and laughed the evening away. One television to 10 rowdy fans added to the excitement. That was the first time I met Tom, though I had heard Benny and Sarah speak about him on numerous occasions in the past, Tom and I had never had the opportunity to actually meet." Margaret's hallucinations had transported her back inside the house, snuggled under her favorite pink flannel quilt, propped up by two fluffy pillows, reading a book.

"It was pre-game time as we all huddled in the kitchen sampling the latest concoction. When Tom arrived, Benny made a quick announcement and introduction at the door, I followed Sarah to the front room and greeted Tom and the other arrivers, and then returned to the kitchen to help mix and fix. I really didn't pay much attention to Tom there were so many people there it seemed we all had one goal, showing our moral support by cheering for our favorite team, and discussing winning strategies." Margaret's lips could no longer functioned to form her words, her thoughts raced back and forth to indiscriminate events.

"Enjoyable, funny with a sense of humor, Tom was the perfect match. We both enjoyed sports and especially football games. We were both active in intramural sports on campus and liked being around other people. We knew that we enjoyed being with each other.

"Tom was my first love. We had fun, there were the meetings at the library, we studied together. Tom would quiz me and help me get ready for my exams. I loved the times we would spend going to the mall shopping, and then there were the poetry readings and the book store visits. I quickly found that Tom was not a great dancer. Our visits to the local nightclubs and dance clubs were short lived. Tom didn't like dancing much, and we would rather be together than be at the local hangouts. Together we were more academically focused as a unit. Some nights we talked until daybreak. Other times we would cry at a sad movie, holding each other confessing we really didn't like how the movie ended." The fluids from Margaret's nose had also frozen. She could no longer move her head, for it was now sealed to the icy sidewalk.

"Tom and I literally spent hours thumbing through books and talking over coffee. The real fun times were at the civic events, the community causes Tom so much liked to attend, with me tagging along for moral support. Tom always had a voice and a strong opinion about helping others. He had that special zeal for family and human rights. Our first dates were fun filled. That enjoyment continued for the fifty-five years of our marriage. I love you Thomas Steaker. Now where is that fly swatter, the cat is in the baby bird." The snow continued to fall, the wind had picked up again, blowing snow and concealing Margaret's tiny footprints well beneath it.

"Tom and I had been dating for almost two years before we decided to get married. We both wanted to wait until we had graduated from college before we made that commitment. Tom graduated a year before I did, he waited for me to finish and it wasn't long after that Tom and I were married. We were married at the little chapel at Collins College where we both had attended. It was a small baby girl, we knew that she would not live. The lawn needs watering." Margaret's mind would not stay focused. She watched the video of her life play before her with different event popping in and out like a slide show production.

"Tom, a biology major, had applied for a position with Kendon Research and Development Center. We had decided that if he did get hired there we would relocate to the nearest town and make a go of it. When he did get the call it was just two months before I was to graduate. I had majored in English literature and quickly got a job at Dyden's Book and Coffee Shop, one of the largest chain of bookstores in the region. It was not far from where Tom worked. Sometimes we would meet for a quick lunch when time permitted. It worked out well, for we would ride together to work and returned together each day."

Margaret recollected her thoughts and began her lonely conversation again. "I hope I remembered to turn the water sprinkler off, the lawn is looking just a bit dried and the grass has turned brown this summer. I think this is possibly the hottest summer that I can remember out of all the years that we have lived here. 'Honey, don't you think so? Tom! Tom! Is the sprinkler hooked up?'

"I'll never forget our wedding day. I had just graduated from college with a degree in English, we both had little time to tell all our friends and family. Our wedding was in the University Chapel. It was a very small, quaint event and good thing, I almost tripped on the carpet as I was coming down the aisle. I really did have to hold on to my dad's arm. Daddy! Daddy! Michael said I look ugly in my new dress, he hid it and won't give it back to me!" Margaret tried unsuccessfully to lift her hand. She was delirious.

"Mom and Dad were kind of indifferent to Tom and I getting married. They were happy that we did wait until we both had our careers on track. I guess Mom was happy for me. She could see all the good that I saw in Tom. It took years for Dad to get used to his baby girl being married. I was Dad's little princess for a long time before my younger sister was born. I think it is one thing for your son to get married and another thing for your oldest daughter to get married.

"Tom and I had a pretty big wedding reception. There were over a hundred people there. Our family, friends and school mates came to the Student Union Reception Room and celebrated with us. We had hired 'Crazy Jimmy' to be the disc jockey and we also had Johnny and Terry the musical duo play dance music. They really kept the floor hopping. I can remember we stayed up all night that night, dancing and visiting with friends and family. The next day we began packing for our move to Tipton.

"It was funny, we did not unpack our wedding gifts until after we had been living in Tipton two months. Our honeymoon was delayed, because of the move, but we managed to get away to the Florida Keys for a week that following year." Margaret's thoughts drifted to the ocean, and walking along the beach hand-in-hand with Tom.

"Being newly weds was great, not only did we have a new house, we had a lot of new appliances and household accessories. It was great, we received a lot of things we needed settling in a new home. Every gift was really appreciated. My Aunt Jen gave us a basket filled with canned foods and box mixes. The food really came in handy for those days we were still unpacking. It took me forever it seems to send out the thank you cards. I realized then that I just hate packing and moving, everything is in such disarray while living out of boxes." Margaret's thoughts stopped momentarily, she could not remember what she was talking about.

"For the first few years of marriage Tom and I were in bliss, it was much like we never stopped dating. Many weekends were spent at the library, bookstores, comedy shows and a large variety of activities and community events. There was always something to keep us occupied. Being young and in love, means you want to spend time together, and you both enjoy being together." Margaret could barely hear the muffled sounds of the wind, as it played tag with the various rooftops.

"That was the beginning of an interesting 55 years of marriage with ups and downs, laughter, tears, and a loving relationship that produced three beautiful sons: Bill, Jesse, and Edward."

Margaret looked at the snow formations on each branch of the shrubs that had been planted in front of the front room picture window. The same spruce shrub also bordered one side of the walkway. The weight of the snow had bent and folded the spruce-like branches causing each to succumb to the culmination of weight each tiny snowflake had contributed to that end. The forceful wind rattled the shrub's branches causing small piles of snow to fall and join the blanket of snow that had covered everything.

"We had moved to Tipton just 10 miles from Everton. Tom had landed a good job with Kendon Research in Everton, Illinois. We uprooted from a bustling college town and relocated to the quaint suburb of Tipton. We have been here in Tipton every since. At first we lived on the west side of Tipton a hotel, until we closed on the house. Sometimes Tom and I would take a weekend getaway and stay at that hotel, Willow Mannor on the northwest side of Tipton." The snow pressed unforgivingly against Margaret's partially closed eyelids. She could not remember where she was, nor that she was dying at that very moment.

"The cute, small-framed house with two bedrooms and one bath we first looked at just was not what we wanted. One bath just wasn't enough so we looked at other places. Tom and I both agreed we needed space. We moved to the far north side of Tipton in a four bedroom house. At first we had planned to use two of the upstairs bedrooms for office space, library and exercise rooms, then after the boys came along we found that we needed the rooms for bedrooms. Our little family was rapidly expanding. The four bedrooms, a bath and a-half, brick, two story house was the one we liked best. This was our home. Tom and I love the neighborly feeling people around here have. I guess that is why we have been living in this area for the past 52 years. We had our kids here and raised our family here." Margaret had no clue where she was or where 'here' was. The wind chill factor had caused a surge in temperatures. It was now a frigid 15 below zero, exposed flesh can freeze in less than a minute in the brutal cold.

X

"I was working at the Dyden bookstore when I first found out that I was pregnant with our first child. I can remember I could hardly wait for Tom to get off work that evening, so I called him on the job and shared the news. We both were so excited. I can remember Tom wanting to be fully settled into our new life and home before we planned the arrival of our first child. The timing was perfect, and after two years of marriage, I found myself pregnant, expecting our first child. We both were so happy then. There was a great sense of excitement.

"With Tom and I both working it was hard not to be selfish with our time together. There were many times the two of us spent sipping a cup of tea or coffee around the kitchen table discussing thoughts we had.

"With Tom working a good job, and me part-time we had plenty of time for making the best of our marriage. We had bought a nice little house, and now the arrival of our first baby, I could not have been happier.

"I can remember when Tom and I were expecting our first new addition to the family. We pretty much knew or rather guessed that it was a little girl, we had planned and prepared for this little one. Tom and I both felt it was time to have a family. The joy and expectations, Tom and I knew that it was time. We were totally ready to welcome this little one into our lives.

"It was a humid Sunday afternoon in June of 1955, Tom and I had just returned from church worship services. I can remember it so clearly, we put together an excellent meal that day. That is one thing we enjoyed, cooking, working and doing things together. We had finished a wonderful meal of grilled steaks, and Tom's favorite, shrimp kabobs. The warming sun pierced the misty humid air. Sunset would end this day and find us sitting on the back screened-in porch. We watched the glowing sky silhouette the tree line of summer foliage in the distance. Tom and I thought we had a real deal when we bought this house. The porch was an addition we made before Samantha Ann or the kids came along. We had practically spent every weekend that past August building that porch. We shared a lot of special memories there. It was a place to sit and contemplate hot summer evenings while enjoying the summer breezes and the perfect place to discuss the good news, that I was expecting our first child. I told Tom I was a little scared.

"Samantha Ann was our first child, she was special, and besides we never had another girl. Don't get me wrong, I loved having and raising three boys, but girls are special and different. She was so tiny, 6 pounds 7 ounces. I looked forward to having Samantha, the things we would do, the things that I would teach her. Samantha Ann lived for two minutes thirty-two seconds. The doctor let me dress her in the clothes I had brought along to take her home from the hospital. Tom and I both got to hold and cradle her a moment before they took her out of the room. Tom and I shared the excitement, besides, it is not like we could change the course of nature. If you know what I mean." The snow had totally engulfed Margaret. With a glazed fixed stare, she peered at a blanket of "crystal whiteness."

"The craving of different types of food was an adjustment for me. In the past, I had never really eaten very many peanut butter and jelly sandwiches on whole wheat with bananas, until I was pregnant. Then I craved them. Tom was wonderful and understanding for late night cravings of ice cream and dill pickles. He even tried to keep extra treats that I seemed to crave on board in the pantry. I could not ask for a better man. He is so supportive of me. We never really argued, we both would just speak our piece and go our way and not keep hashing over and over a tough issue." Margaret's brain seemed to stop processing for a brief moment.

"Another big adjustment was the restriction of activity, I found there are a lot of things a pregnant woman just can't do. I couldn't see my feet for months. One day I walked out of the house with a blue shoe on the left foot and a black shoe on the right. I was definitely swollen and disfigured. I had bought a whole new wardrobe of maternity clothes. Besides, nothing that I already had to wear seemed to fit comfortably. I can still remember the fascination of feeling the first movements of a child I was carrying. Hiccups, arm and foot movements create a unique sensation inside a pregnant woman. I can remember going to bed, waking up frequently to accommodate necessary needs I knew that love was growing inside me.

"When my first child did not make it, I was lost. There is the blame, the shame, the constant thought of, 'what ifs.' I had carried this child for nearly eight months and now my doctors were recommending the fetus be aborted and terminate the pregnancy. We chose to follow the doctor's recommendation and terminate the pregnancy and that decision would be one that will always present the question, 'what if?' for me." Margaret's thoughts shifted.

"It was so different with the boys. Tom and I were much more relaxed and better able to calmly deal with calamities. All three were easy pregnancies and I had no problems with any of the boys. All three were happy, healthy babies. The trauma that we went through with our first child had well prepared us for what to expect with the boys.

"Childbirth was a real experience, each time is one to remember. I was in labor for fifteen hours with Samantha Ann, eleven hours with Bill, and eight with Jesse. By the time little Edward came along the time spent in actual labor had decreased significantly. There is a definite pain that a woman goes through to bring a child into this world. It is almost unbearable. Childbirth takes a woman to the furthest degree of reality. I can remember my mom telling me that 'child birth is the closest a woman comes to death.' After the events that I went through with our first child I would tend to agree with what Mom said." Margaret tried hopelessly to move her right index finger, but it would not respond to her command.

"I hope I remembered to turn the coffee maker off this morning. That is something that I have been working on. Lately I have been leaving the coffee maker on. I think it is because I got a new one about six months ago. This new coffeemaker just doesn't work like the old one did. This new one, you can program it to have your coffee fixed when you get out of bed. Dorothy Leggins at church has one just like it. She recommended this model, she says she likes it a lot and it has coffee ready and waiting for her when she gets out of bed each morning. I have never been able to figure out how to program the coffee maker just right to do all that it is supposed to do.

"Tom and I both felt we were ready to be parents. We both looked forward to the new addition to our family. Unfortunately our first child, a little girl, had to be aborted after the second trimester. The baby girl that I was carrying was developing without a functioning heart and would not be able to survive outside the womb. The doctors realized the problems and immediately suggested an abortion.

"That was a difficult time for Tom and I. Making the decision to terminate the pregnancy was against everything we both believed. But the problem was more that the child could not circulate blood without a functioning heart. This was our first child, and she was not going to have a chance to live, grow or be who she was. Tom stayed by my side through the whole ordeal. For a long time I blamed myself and found it hard to communicate my true feeling about losing the child. I always wondered if there was something I had done wrong during the pregnancy." Margaret could not feel her body shaking in violent muscle spasms.

"I have not seen that navy blue scarf that Bill sent me from Paris when he went there for part of his aviation training. I thought I had put it in the drawer with my other hats. I guess I didn't. I really liked that scarf a lot. In fact it is one of my favorites. It really blocks the wind. Over the years I have found that I need something covering my ears and a hat especially in the winter. My hair has thinned considerably and now I catch cold when I don't wear my scarf or something on my head.

"I always think back on our first child, our little girl. Samantha Ann was the name that I called her, she would be a year or so older than Bill our oldest son. I think that any woman that has to go through the trauma of abortion or losing a child never really forgets that child or the initial experience of being pregnant. I think about Samantha Ann's birthday, how it might have been, her first day of school, what she would grow up to be. I have never forgotten her, I don't think I ever will. Tom and I never had another girl, but the three boys all but made up for it." Margaret thought she was crying. Her eyes were hurting from the thin layer of ice, now freezing her pupils.

"A year after the abortion, little Billy came along and before we knew it, our little family had begun to grow. I was determined to do everything right. I wanted this child to live a normal, healthy life. I quit my job at Dyden's and became a full-time mom. I exercised and stayed on a well balanced diet. I avoided stressful situations and was happy to be a homemaker for Tom and the new baby."

Margaret's thoughts raced to the house, "Yes this house is too big for just one person. I might just consider moving into a smaller place with less up-keep. Since the kids are gone, and with Tom gone too, there is no need for me to try to keep this house up next year. I think it may be time to consider downsizing. I don't want to worry about finding someone to mow the grass next month." Margaret's mind jumped back and forth in time.

"I can still remember the Belmont Junior and Senior Prom. I was a junior and that was actually the first real dress-up event that I had ever attended in my life. I was allowed to wear make-up, heels, and stockings that evening. Kenny Minton asked me if I would go with him to the prom. I can remember so well, it was between classes, I had just come from English class. I was on my way to Home Economics when he asked. Traditionally upperclassmen got to class early, dropped off their books and personal belongings, and then hung at the doorway until the bell rang.

"I thought I was going to die. Kenny just walked up to me and asked me while I was standing by the classroom doorway. I was wearing a blue and white pin-striped dress with a navy collar. That dress made me look five pounds thinner. It was one of my favorites. I had a real good time with Kenny, he was a real gentleman. I wonder what ever happened to him. After we graduated he went into the military and moved to California.

"Tom and I didn't plan for Jesse or Edward, but were both a welcomed addition to our family. All three boys were born so close together, it was almost like having triplets. There were advantages to having the boys so close together, for one thing you can easily recycle clothes and baby ware. You can buy some things in bulk, like diapers, and bottles. You can put them all on the same nap schedule, which gives you a little time to catch up on other household chores. Having two children in diapers at the same time can be an endless demand on time." With that Margaret tried to tuck her legs into a fetal position, but the broken hip remained fixated to the frozen sidewalk.

"As the boys grew, the age difference dissipated. Bill, Jesse and Edward were playmates and the best of friends. They were brothers who took up for each other and shared in the joys and disappointments that growing boys go through. When one wanted to try out for the basketball team the other two were there to give their support. Each of the boys was different in their own special way. Bill the oldest was adventuresome, he was always trying new things. It was funny to watch as Jesse and Edward tried to follow in Bill's path. When Bill first learned how to ride a bicycle, it wasn't long before Jesse tried his hand at it too, with Edward quickly following." A warm tingling feeling started in the tip of Margaret's left foot and slowly worked its way up the length of her body. She could not recognize the sensation of severe pain mixed with acute hypothermia.

"Tom and I always played an active role in the schools, where the boys attended. We went to the school programs, sent treats for special occasions, and were coach parents for the Little League. I was den mother for the Scouts and Tom was a Scout Leader." Margaret reflected back to the times when the boys were young.

"One of my most memorable times was when Tom and I took twelve little boys camping at Lake Winnipeg for their first camping experience. That was truly an adventure. Setting up tents, gathering firewood and being prepared for whatever was testing the skills of each participant. We had loaded the van and the car with enough supplies to endure the four-day trek. The washing machine is on the rinse cycle now. Glancing in the rearview mirror reflected smiling faces of young Scouts ready for an adventure." Margaret's thoughts drifted.

In a whispery voice Margaret continued, "The Johnsons were always there to assist with the troop's activities. Harold and Peggy Johnson also drove their two vehicles loaded with supplies and kids too. They were great chaperones for camping trips as such. Their son Toby Johnson was 11 years old, the same age as our son Jesse. Toby and Jesse were friends for life, they attended the same school, were in the same classes and shared in many activities as best buddies. Toby grew up and moved to Chicago to study acting."

Margaret summoned a faint smile to her near frozen face. "Our Scout camping trips proved to be a great time for discovery. I discovered that some little boys are just as afraid of spiders and snakes as much as I was as a little girl. Then there were those who were afraid of the dark, they had trouble sleeping the first couple of nights. Other little boys had never really caught fish from the lake, or been fishing for that matter and had trouble taking their meager catch from the hook. Yet there were some who had never been away from home, this was their first time to be away from mommy and daddy. They were immensely homesick." Margaret thought she was staring directly into the headlights of an oncoming vehicle.

For a moment Margaret remembered her favorite smells. She paused, savored a moment, and then returned to her preview of lifetime events. "There is nothing like the smell of fire wood burning in an open campfire coupled with hot dogs skewing on 'make-shift branched' skewing stick. The boys were responsible for cooking their own hot dogs. There was the occasional burnt hot dog, but for the most part they all proved to be survivalists. The open fire, hot dogs, and marshmallows were always enjoyed by all. The boys practiced skits for the late night campfire at which they would present stories, songs and skits they had managed to make up earlier during the day. Those were the days, I'll tell you, we really had some good times.

"We always limited the scary stories so the younger ones would not be too scared to sleep. Then there was 'kick-can-ice-cream.' That was interesting, making homemade ice cream in coffee cans. I could tell that there was some doubt as to whether or not you could actually make ice cream that way, but it worked. It was fun to sample the different flavors that each pair of boys conjured up. Chocolate chip was one of my favorites, but the banana was exceptionally good too. Personally I mixed the two for a banana split taste. Our summer camping trips with the Scouts were something to remember." Margaret tried desperately to touch her fingers to her mouth. She had no sensation in her limbs. She only imaged the warmth of the campfire against her face and Tom slipping his jacket on her shoulders.

"Family picnics were especially fun. Tom and I would gather the boys and take off for who knows where for a day of family fun. One of our favorite parks, White Water, was about 25 miles away. I would fix Sunday dinner picnic style, and after church we would head for White Water for an afternoon of fun, food and outdoor activities. I had always made it a habit to pack extra food for the kids' friends who happened by the picnic table. One Sunday we went through two whole chickens I had fried up, a bucket of potato salad, baked beans and two bags of chips before the day ended. Another time we grilled out, and cooked hot dogs for all the kids playing softball. A couple of wives sent their husbands back into town to get more hot dogs, buns and chips. That was an event to remember, it reminded me of our Scout camp outs. We roasted marshmallows over the hot coals before we left for home." Margaret thought of her family, and how happy her life had been. She also thought about all the newborn infants she had seen over the years, at St. Mary's.

"White Water Park was where most people of Tipton ended up going to on Sundays. It was more like the local community gathering place for us all. I would visit with neighbors exchanging the latest recipes or sewing ideas while Tom entertained the boys. Sometimes the boys would play with schoolmates, and other neighborhood children who happened to be at the park that day. Tom would bring along games which usually included the softball, bat, catcher mitts, and get a softball game going. I can remember the first time Jesse hit a home run, you would have thought we were at a national ball game, with all the parents and siblings clapping and cheering. Jesse didn't know which way to run, but Tom coached him around to each base. That home run was one of the highlights of that day. I was so proud of Jesse, I knew how much he wanted to be able to hit the ball. This was the first time Jesse had been a star hitter." A feeble smile appeared on Margaret's face.

With flutters of snowflakes swirling all around landing lightly about, Margaret blinked her eyes at the snow and thought, "Then there was the time when little Edward got stuck at the top of the slide at White Water. With me standing at the bottom with open arms, worried sick, Tom went up the ladder and slid down with a smiling little Edward. After that Edward was no longer afraid to go up and down by himself. That was nothing compared to the time when Bill jumped out of the swing, only to hurt his ankle. We spent the rest of that day in the emergency room at the hospital. The doctor said Bill had a serious sprained ankle and he would have to wear a cast for a few weeks until his ankle healed. Before we knew it, the cast was off and Bill was back to his old self. Those were just a few of the wonderful times we shared together as a family." Margaret realized that her eyes did not move when she tried to close them. They were frozen, half-shut, half-open, fixated and lifeless.

"One of my hardest times was little Bill's first day of school. This was our first child to go off into the big world. Bill was old enough to start first grade, he was a big seven years old. I can remember he was so excited, but I was nervous and worried. I guess that comes with the territory of being a parent. Now, Bill would be riding the bus that passed by daily picking up other neighborhood school kids. The boys and I had watched the big yellow school bus pass the house daily. It was more like a ritual to peer out the front picture window to see the loading and unloading of neighborhood children." As hard as she tried, Margaret could not lift her head from the frozen concrete.

"The boys and I had watched the bus come and go for years, and now our Bill would be one of the children getting on and off the bus as it stopped. I can remember we had planned and rehearsed the event over and over. I reminded Bill to sit up front, behind the bus driver, to be nice, to stay seated until the bus stopped at the school's loading zone, and to stand back from the sidewalk curb until the bus came to a complete stop. By the time I stopped worrying about Bill's school adventures, Jesse was due to start. Now I had two of my babies getting on the big yellow school bus."

Margaret tried to remember what day it was but couldn't. Her thoughts and mind was clouded. "The first few weeks were particularly trying for me with two of the boys gone. A few mornings I found myself sitting on the front porch with little Edward waving bye to his brothers and the big yellow school bus, as tears flowed freely down my face. I also discovered how difficult it was trying to entertain little Edward, while the boys were off to school. I had to relearn how to play with toy trucks, and action figures. It was our special time for bonding, and that is what we did. My how time passes, all the kids are grown now, with kids of their own.

"Edward was an interesting child. He was so much like his big brothers, but yet he had retained a bit of innocence that the older two had somehow outgrown. I felt there was so much to learn about him and so little time, for I realized that the next year, little Edward too would be leaving for his first day of school. I knew from my experiences with the older boys that this was the last year Edward would be home with me. From that point I tried to make every day special, for I knew he would soon be off to school with his brothers. I could easily tell that Edward missed the company of his older brothers and could hardly wait each day for their return." Margaret did not recognize where she was, nor could she remember what she was doing there. The snow offered a warm blanket that shrouded her from the cold wind. Margaret felt warm and comfortable.

"With our first two boys in school, Tom and I found that we had immersed ourselves in the kids' school activities and events. Those were special times. I can remember when we all packed up to go to the annual school spring festival. Bill had a lead part in the play, and Jesse would be singing a solo. During the program our little Edward yelled, 'That's my brother. Hi Bill. And there's Jesse, Mommy.' You could hear laughter throughout the auditorium. It was a bit embarrassing for both boys, even though Tom and I saw it as humorous. Edward had said it with great sincerity." Margaret tried to scream, for she had momentarily loss and regained consciousness again. The sudden darkness had frightened her.

"It was tough when Edward started first grade. I guess it was the first realization of the 'empty nest syndrome' for me. Now I found myself at home alone, wondering how the boys' school day would unfold. The morning breakfasts, the lunch bags, and the backpacks; morning always seemed so hurried and chaotic just making sure all the guys had their homework, matching socks, coats, backpacks, and school projects ready to go. It is truly a chore, now especially with all three in school. After school, when the kids arrived, always seemed like a time of reckoning for me. There were the teacher notes and other correspondence that had to be found. I usually had to search all three backpacks, retrieving school work, papers, teacher notes, to see what was new, what was due, and determine when school conferences were scheduled." Margaret could not feel any sensation in her legs. She did not notice the sporadic muscle twitches from either.

"I will admit there were times when I was hesitant to reach my bare hand into Bill's backpack for fear some crawly little creature would emerge. Bill was my nature boy. He had a strong desire to know and explore creepy crawly things. I can remember the time Bill had a baby garter snake lodged in the deep corner of his backpack. You can't image me screaming through the house, as the little creature slithered through my fingers and fell back into his pack." Margaret thought what it was like to have a snake slither through her fingers, her eyes half open, were fixed silently in a deathly gaze. Her mind was the only functioning part that remained.

"Jesse always seemed to have some leftover food bits or half eaten snacks in his backpack. One day, I remember he had an old baloney sandwich he had left in his desk the week before. He had just stuffed it into his backpack and brought it home. The hard, crusty bread and a dried piece of baloney were not a welcoming sight to fish from a kid's backpack. The bread had crumbled into pieces, and I could hardly recognize what the baloney was it was so shriveled and looked like a piece of rubber. Now I can only laugh at those days. I must admit, there was never a dull moment raising three boys, they were always so full of life and crazy antics. I never knew what to expect, and learned not to be surprised or overreact at anything they did. They were healthy, curious growing boys." Margaret's thoughts drifted to her infant daughter who died.

"They all seemed to change as they grew. Later Bill developed his love for aviation. Jesse became a musician and Eddy became a biologist. I guess they picked it up from each other. What Bill was once interested in, Edward later studies and vice verse. You are never really sure what a person will grow up to be." Margaret entertained the thoughts of becoming a fashion designer, her true career desire, which was never realized. For a brief moment Margaret felt cold and angry. Her mind flashed back to Tom's chemo treatments at St. Mary's.

"The boys' high school days presented even more challenges. When Bill first entered high school as a freshman, much of my time was spent chauffeuring him to and from sporting events, science fairs, and after school activities. That was when Jesse and Edward were still in middle school, so between the three of them the van stayed in overdrive. I was either picking one of the boys up, or dropping another one off some place. It was a hectic time, but even so much more, when all three boys were in high school. Fortunately for me, Bill had gotten his drivers license and was more than willing to take his little brothers where they need to go. Bill was really a big help with things like that. I was happy that he had proved to be a safe driver and was eager to drive to and from all the events and activities his little brothers were involved in." Margaret thought of the nights she sat up, or stayed awake in bed, waiting for one of the boys to come home. She recaptured the worried feelings she had about each of them driving late at night. Margaret sincerely wondered if dads had those same worries.

"Thinking back it was harder for me to accept the fact that Jesse was growing up and Edward too. When Jesse had gotten his drivers license I was afraid to let him drive alone. Even so a year later when little Edward started to drive, I realized that all the boys would soon be starting their own lives and growing into manhood. Tom and I soon realized that we needed an extra car in the family now that the boys were old enough to drive." Margaret felt a warm, tingling sensation in her lower extremities. She tried unsuccessfully to roll over onto her left side. The struggle ceased.

"I hope I remembered to turn off the coffee maker this evening.

That is one thing with living alone, you have to double-check yourself. I have a terrible time remembering to turn off the coffeepot each morning. I having been planning to get one of the automatic drip coffee makers, the kind that automatically shuts itself off after being on for an hour. I can't remember if I did or did not turn it off this morning." Hypothermia had taken its toll on Margaret's frail body.

Margaret's thinking had become clouded and confused. "I hope I fixed the kids' lunches before I left, they always want to know what kind of sandwiches I put in their lunch bags the night before I fix them. I know they all like tuna salad, all but little Edward, he would just soon eat a peanut butter and jelly sandwich any day as to have tuna salad. I put an apple, and a bag of chips in each lunch bag. I signed that note Jesse's teacher sent home yesterday. I have to remember to pick up Bill from soccer practice. I hope Edward remembers to bring his homework assignments home. This is Christmas break weekend and he will have to catch up with his school work."

Margaret was disoriented and confused. "I hope that the newborns like the little quilts I just finished making. Of course they will, infants don't really notice what they are dressed in. The little pink quilt will go to the new premature little girl, Samantha Ann. I hope Samantha Ann has a nice day her first day of school. She really doesn't look much like Tom or me. It is funny how you think your first child should look like one or the other parent. Daddy! Daddy! Willy put a spider on me. London Bridge is falling down, falling down, my little lollipop.

"I think Julie scheduled my next hair appointment for next Saturday. I really need to get my perm touched up. I was thinking of maybe having her dye my hair a bit. I would not get it dyed too dark, but I think that auburn highlights might look pretty good. One of the gals down at the senior center had Julie do her hair that way and it turned out pretty good. I don't want to have it dyed too dark, it would look unnatural. Just a few highlights will do it. I thought I might have her do my nails too while I am there. The boys' dentist appointments are today. I feel lightheaded. The Easter egg hunt is tomorrow…" Margaret drifted in and out of consciences.

Margaret began to nod off in a sleep-like state. She mumbled, "Tom said he wanted to wear his blue and red tie tomorrow. I can't seem to remember where it is. He has a big meeting with the international distributors. He really likes to wear that blue and red tie with his dark blue suit. Aunt Julie will be at the airport tomorrow. Tom always looks so nice when he dresses in that dark blue suit. He wasn't sure he would like it for a summer suit. Hey! Hey! You are hurting him. I can't breathe! It's wet! I'm wet! Can you hear me? It's cold there! That was the one that the kids and I bought him when he was promoted to manager of his division. He likes his pinstriped gray one too. I think that blue and red tie is in the second lefthand drawer in the dresser. The boys will be visiting for the New Year's Holiday this year. I will have to look and find it. I know he really wants to wear it tomorrow. I feel like my eyes are glued shut. La..la…la…de…No man is and island, we all would agree sing ye now my baby. La..la..la. The Hills are alive with the sound of raindeeeeeer da…da.da…dada…d…I'm floating…I'm floating… I'm sleepy, it's hot in here." Margaret's hallucinations seemed real. She floated freely in and out of consciousness.

"I am going to call Mom later today and see if she and Dad are still coming to visit next week. They always try to come to spend a couple of weeks with us each summer. At first they didn't really like Tom and me being married. Mom thought I would marry Henry Sutton. Henry and I grew up together and were high school sweet hearts. We went our different ways after high school. Henry went away to Chicago to school and I ended up in the southern part of the state. We didn't keep in touch much after high school, but Mom always kept me posted on what he was doing. Mom was good friends with Mrs. Sutton and the two traded stories daily. It never surprised me when I did by chance see Henry, for he was always up-to-date on all the events in my life." Margaret, delirious and worn, was falling into a deep sleep, as she mumbled.

"I was born Margaret Elizabeth Straton, originally from a small town, Williamsburg, Indiana. I was the third child of four. I had two older brothers, Michael and William respectively, and one younger sister, Susan…I was born the third child to Mary and James Straton of Williamsburg, Indiana. My dad worked for the railroad, and in those

FIVE FEET

days believe me, that was considered, top of the line employment. I attended the local elementary and high school. In Williamsburg, everyone knew everyone, it is pretty much small town living there. It was a big surprise when I left for college in another state. Most kids I graduated with went to the local Williamsburg Community College for a two-year degree and then found local jobs, many carrying on the family business or work in rural agricultural business. My two brothers still live in Williamsburg. My brother Michael the oldest has three children by his second wife and my brother William has two children." Margaret drifted in and out of a deep sleep, repeating conversations she had told before.

Margaret thought of the numerous times she and Tom would help out at the various school activities while the boys were growing up. "When the boys went to their Junior-Senior Proms, Tom and I were there as parent helpers. It was sort of funny seeing your kids all dressed up and grown up, knowing that they would soon be graduating from high school. Chaperoning at the prom was very special for Tom and I. It was very much like going to our prom back in high school and college. That was a very romantic time for me. Hey guys, the bus just turned the corner. Sam Jacobson passed away today. I just hope Mom will let me wear my new green dress.

"I haven't been back to Williamsburg for a while. I still get Christmas cards from them each year. Each week we take the kids to the Easter Egg Hunt at the park at 2:00 on New Years Day. Tom and I tried to go each year and take the kids. I guess William, my youngest brother, has had a lot of trouble getting his blue coat in the oven, with his youngest son getting into trouble. The courts gave him fifteen years for an armed robbery that they claimed he was in was in the swimming pool. I hear the boy drove his friends to Colorado, and they went in and robed the store while William's boy waited outside the baby's daiper, thinking his friends went in for sodas. He was in the wrong place at the wrong time, and ended up losing fifteen years of his life for it. Now, he can't have ice cream or tick-or-treat."

Margaret's thoughts jumped to her next doctor's appointment. She was trying to remember if it was scheduled for a Tuesday or Thursday.

At that moment she felt it was very important that she check her schedule to see when she had made that appointment for.

Margaret's life passed before her, like a fast forward rerun. Events were only fragments of her memory. "My oldest brother Michael is expecting his seventh grandchild. His daughter is due to give birth sometime at the pharmacy. Willy, Eddy, Jesse, Tom, Michael has been the one to keep the family name going with so many sons, he just has the one daughter. Little Eddy, is her name, she married a fellow out of New York. I was surprised that a person from prison would settle for living in Williamsburg Indiana, but now I see the attraction, of a big city person, moving to a small town, amusement park. Tom, would you please turn on the air conditioner? I can't reach the telephone cord." Margaret did not know where she was, how long she had been there, or if it was day or night.

With heavy eyelids, and cuddling her raincoat she muttered. "I don't know why Bill brought a little puppy home yesterday. He said that it followed him home. He had already given it a name. Duke; what a strong name for such a little fluff ball. We weren't sure what Duke was mixed with. I think he is part German Shepard and Lab mixed. By the size of his paws, I think he is going to be big whatever breed he is. Tom and the boys built Duke a little doghouse and fixed a place for him in the backyard. They are planning to have him checked by the vet tomorrow."

Thoughts continued to randomly appear in Margaret's mind. "I wonder if Tom is going to pick up Edward from basketball practice tonight. I think it is Tuesday and I know that Bill will be helping with the Junior-Senior Prom, and I can't remember where Jesse will be tonight. I think he is going to a friend's house to study for his Social Studies test that he has on Friday. I better call Tom and make sure. What time is it?" Margaret felt tired, and sleepy. She wanted to yawn but lacked the energy, besides it was rather comfortable there.

Margaret tried to remember if she had a hair appointment this week. It was as if she could not concentrate on things clearly. She ran the thoughts over and over in her mind but could not come to a consensus when her next hair appointment was. She thought it might be today, but was not for certain. She began to worry that she would be late for the beauty salon. She knew that she needed a perm and a conditioner soon.

"The telephone repairman will be here later today to install a new line upstairs for the boys. It has been so hectic with the boys growing up and using the phone. Guys will you bring your dirty laundry to the church. Hurry we will be late. When they are home, there is always one of them on the phone. Sometime ago Tom and I decided to get them their own phone line. That way we can still use the main line to make and receive phone calls." Margaret felt excited that the boys would have their very own telephone upstairs. "That would stop the need for them to run down the stairs each time the phone rang. I found that blue shoe behind the staircase just the other day.

Margaret could feel delayed pain in her hip and leg. "My leg hurts. I am not sure why. I think I have a cramp or something in it. The pain is almost unbearable. I wonder if it is from going up and down the stairs to the kids' rooms. I have to go and retrieve dirty clothes or put away the kids' laundry. I hope Bill remembered to feed the gold fish this morning. He really needs to clean that fish bowl. Funny I have to remind him to do that, Bill usually is very responsible. I should have one of the boys take out the trash since today is Sunday. Ring around the rosey, a pocket full of toasty, bacon, turkey, we all fall down, and can't get up!

"I hope there is enough milk in the fridge for the kids' breakfast tomorrow. We go through a gallon every two days. I try to buy three gallons a week, but even with that it seems that sometimes we run out right in the middle of the week. I better call Tom and tell him to bring a gallon home tonight after work. Tom is good about calling to see what we need at the hospital before he leaves the office. Tom has always been so helpful with the kids and me. He is a real family man. I really lucked out marrying a good man like Tom. I can't think what it would be like being married to anyone else. I have to be at the school tonight for the play. Jesse has the lead role." Margaret had forgotten that she was dying and slowly freezing to death. She had found comfort in her thoughts.

"I guess I will fix that roast tonight for dinner. I took it out of the freezer and put it in the fridge, it should be thawed and ready to start baking. I think I will put potatoes and carrots in while it's baking. That is one thing we all agree on, roast beef with vegetables. Guys, the bus is here. Hurry, Jesse. I usually fix the easy bake dinner rolls and a toss salad as side dishes. Everyone seems to agree on my meatloaf too. The repairman will be here for the water heater later today. I mix two pounds of ground beef, with a pound of sausage, three cups of breadcrumbs two egg and seasonings. I fix a gravy mixture to pour over the top. I used to put a tomato sauce on top, but I found the kids don't like the tomato sauce so now I just fix meatloaf with gravy. The Fourth of July fireworks are tonight at dusk. I want the boys to get their pictures taken with Santa at the mall later this week." The blanket of snow seemed to encase Margaret's tiny body and shield it from the harshness of the wind. She felt peaceful.

In and out of consciousness she drifted. "I loved Tom Steaker. He and I shared a wonderful life together. We were married for the past, now let me see, Tom has been dead for three or, is it four years. If Tom were still living it would be our 55 years that we have been together. That was the timer on the clothes dryer. Did you hear that? Is that the seatbelt bell ringing? From the first time we met, there was a 'click.' We knew that we were made for each other. We had a beautiful married life together. I could not ask for more in a marriage. Tom was a great father to the boys too." A beaming smile appeared on Margaret's blue lips. The cold was taking its toll on the 79-year-old. She could not hang on much longer, even though her thoughts continued to materialize.

"Maybe we should eat out tonight. We have a local family restaurant, Grandma's Kubbard, that we love to go to. They serve family style, or buffet style. We just love it, everyone can order what they want to eat with out the hustle-bustle. This has been a hot summer, and any excuse to get out of the kitchen is fair. It is just too hot to cook. I guess I could call Tom and see if he wants to have pizza delivered tonight. That is one thing the boys will all agree on, pizza. I usually order a pepperoni and sausage party size and fix a toss salad and there you have it, the quick meal sure to please everyone. Where is the telephone book? I can't seem to remember the name or phone number of that pizza delivery guy, the one, the one with the red hair, and the little blue car. Oh, he goes to school with Bill, now what's his name? This year's fireworks are the best, just look at all those bright lights, how beautiful. Can you see them?" Margaret was babbling and suffering from hypothermia.

Margaret's thoughts shifted. "I hope I remembered to order the tux for Bill's Senior Prom. I know that it is this Friday. He also wanted me to order flowers for his date. I really like this new girl that he is dating. Tom, that puppy is digging up the flowers, in the fireplace. Bill was so preoccupied with his studies, Tom and I were a little worried. Bill didn't date as much as we thought that he should. He spent little of his time chasing girls. Eventually we realized Bill had set his priorities and that his love for aviation outweighed everything. He was destined to be an air traffic controller. Mommy! Willy hit me, tell him to stop it! That old apple tree needs pruning. Robert Jones is the one who took it, I saw him do it. September first is the last Christmas.

"When we found out that Tom had an incurable cancer, our whole lives changed. We spent numerous hours in the hospital. I watched Tom literally go from a human to a vegetable. It was one of the most difficult times of my life. Eddy got the tickets! Now where is that grocery list? Did you see that? Did you see that? I guess it hurt the most that he didn't know my name or me. My name is Sally Beth Hatcher. Did you hear that? Look there, see it. Did you see that? I live in California. I am a famous fashion designer. Here is the catsup! He had to be fed through a tube that entered his navel. He had to have his intestines rerouted with a colostemytomy and with aspirators. The lymphoma cancer took its toll on us all, it was incurable and quickly rummaged through his 79-year-old body. From the hospital, to the nursing home, to his last days, Tom was more concerned about others and how I would make it without him."

XI

"Tom had lost the struggle for life. Within eight months Tom was gone." Margaret tried unsuccessfully to open her eyes. The cold had set into every part of her body. She no longer had any feeling." Her thoughts began to slowly fade.

"It was hard for me to let go of Tom. After his death, it was like he was still there, I would envision him sitting at the breakfast table talking over his morning cup of coffee. I had visions of him getting in bed each night, how he pulled back the blankets, or adjusted his pillow. The patterns and shape his body made in the dark. The way he said good night, our trips to the refrigerator for late-night snacks. Those special times together are memories I dare not erase, for those were the happiest times of my life. I guess after 52 years of marriage, you start to learn and know that other person you have shared so much of your life with. They are so much a part of your life. Losing Tom like that, seemed like a part of me died along with him. Eddy you are going to miss the bus, hurry get your airplane. A part of you that no one will ever know, for Tom and I had spent the biggest portion of our lives together. If I had it to do all over again, I would not change a thing. I loved my husband and family. I loved the life we had put together. Mommy, Susan's diaper is dirty. Angie Garrett told a lie. I am not! Daddy! Daddy! Mikie called me a 'tattle-tale.' Has anyone seen your dad's keys?"

With a low, faint voice Margaret spoke her last time. "Kids' lunch, get the shoes, pay the utility bills, bring in the groceries, sleepy, buy it's on sale, got to go, that's right, rocking horse, the parent teacher conference, abortion, hot outside, put the dog, just a minute, out of the house, bring the laundry, stop, get in, what for, locked out, you are, wet, red, tree, bite, Santa Claus, truck, lion, baby, socks, nose, cold, be there, bright light. See it…"

Until her words could no longer be heard. The chilling wind silenced her thoughts. The snowflakes swirled in erratic paterns to the ground, endless circles, each flake racing to seek its resting place. With that Margaret Steaker drifted deep into a restful sleep, forever.

XII

Tipton, NEWS WTXC On the Scene News the Weekend Addition, February 13, 2004

Another snowstorm sweeps through Illinois and the Midwest, dropping as much as 2 feet of snow for some residents to dig out. This has been some of the most unseasonable weather since the Blizzard of 2000 with some parts of the East Coast getting as much as 3 to 4 feet of snow within a 24 hour period. As the nation digs out, many businesses, offices, and schools across the state are closed. The Governor of Illinois has declared the southern third of the state to be in a "State of Emergency." Only emergency vehicles will be allowed on the road ways. All unauthorized vehicles will be ticketed. (Reporter Tracey Jones)

FIVE FEET

A Tragic Winter for all Areas in Midwest! Journal Courrier, February 13, 2004
Syndicated News by Ron Whitehouser

TIPTON: There have been 16 reported deaths blamed on the winter snows this year. Another death has occurred closer to home in the Tipton area. It was eight hours ago, on a recent delivery to the resident of Mrs. Margaret Steaker, Leon Welch of Tipton area Postal Services was attempting to deliver special mail to the Steaker residence, when he found the body of 79-year-old, Margaret Steaker frozen in the snow, just a mere five feet from her car Welch said the first thing he spotted is what he thought looked like a human lying in the snow and the thing that caught his eye, was the way she was in the snow. "She looked so peaceful lying there. You couldn't tell what it was. She was completely covered under eight inches of new snow."

Mr. Welch went to the next door neighbor's and called 911 for emergency assistance. EMTs reported that Mrs. Steaker was frozen to the sidewalk and needed firemen to remove the body. The city coroner estimated that Mrs. Steaker had been lying on the sidewalk for nearly two days before she was discovered. Funeral arrangements are pending family notification.

ILLINOIS Courrier Journal, Saturday, February 14, 2004
Weekend Edition (APN Release by Ken Nobbit)
A Tipton Woman Found Five Feet from Automobile

A Tipton woman was found yesterday just a mere five feet from her automobile. Apparently Mrs. Margaret Steaker (79) a life-long resident of Tipton, had a fatal accident on a ice covered walkway as she tried to reach her vehicle parked only five feet from where she met her unlikely fate. Mrs. Steaker's body was found partially snow covered by a postal worker attempting to deliver a special delivery to her address. Leon Welch , mail carrier, reported to local authorities that upon an attempted mail delivery during a visit to the house he saw what looked like a human hand, lying on the side walk. After a closer inspection, Mr. Welch realized it was the body of an elderly woman laying in the snow. An autopsy revealed that Mrs. Steaker had suffered from an apparent broken hip and hyperthermia. Mrs. Steaker had been lying there for possibly two to four days, before being discovered. Several deaths have been attributed to the recent weather. The governor has issued a "State of Emergency" because of the most recent snow storm dropping a record eighteen inches of snow in the Southern Illinois area.

Illinois Daily News
Obituaries

Margaret Straton-Steaker

Margaret E. Straton-Steaker, 79, 1212 N. Madison Heights died on February 11, 2004 at her home in Tipton, Illinois. Born December 12, 1924, in Williamsburg Indiana, to Mary and James Straton. She was a member of the Most Holy Church, Tipton, Illinois. Surviving, are sons; William, Jesse, and Edward Steaker, six grandchildren and two great-grandchildren. She was preceded in death by husband Tom Steaker, and an infant daughter. Services will be 10:00 a.m. Wednesday, February 15, 2004 at Jacobs' Mortuary, with the Rev. Orville Jones officiating. Burial will be at New Heaven Memory Gardens. Friends may call at the mortuary from 7-9 p.m. today and 2-4 p.m. Tuesday.

****

Printed in the United States
17782LVS00001B/94